Khat

The Final Delivery

Suraj Singh Chandraul

Copyright © <2025> <suraj singh chandraul>

All Rights Reserved.

This book has been self-published with all reasonable efforts taken to make the material error-free by the author. No part of this book shall be used, reproduced in any manner whatsoever without written permission from the author, except in the case of brief quotations embodied in critical articles and reviews.

The Author of this book is solely responsible and liable for its content including but not limited to the views, representations, descriptions, statements, information, opinions and references ["Content"]. The Content of this book shall not constitute or be construed or deemed to reflect the opinion or expression of the Publisher or Editor. Neither the Publisher nor Editor endorse or approve the Content of this book or guarantee the reliability, accuracy or completeness of the Content published herein and do not make any representations or warranties of any kind, express or implied, including but not limited to the implied warranties of merchantability, fitness for a particular purpose. The Publisher and Editor shall not be liable whatsoever for any errors, omissions, whether such errors or omissions result from negligence, accident, or any other cause or claims for loss or damages of any kind, including without limitation, indirect or consequential loss or damage arising out of use, inability to use, or about the reliability, accuracy or sufficiency of the information contained in this book.

Made with ❤ on the Notion Press Platform

www.notionpress.com

To Lost and Incomplete Stories

1

Frozen in Time

The wind howled across the mountainside, carrying ice particles that stung Captain Arjun Mehra's exposed face despite the protection of his balaclava. He squinted through his goggles, surveying the treacherous terrain ahead. His reconnaissance team had been navigating these remote Himalayan passes for three days now, mapping potential infiltration routes as part of a routine border security operation.

"Sir, visibility dropping below ten meters," Lieutenant Vikram reported, his voice barely audible over the storm that had intensified in the last hour.

Arjun nodded, checking his GPS coordinates. "We'll make camp in that rock formation ahead. Should provide enough shelter until this passes."

Private Rohit the youngest of their three-man team, looked relieved. Though he'd never complain, the thirteen-hour trek had taken its toll. They'd been pushing hard since dawn, and the March weather in these elevations was unforgiving.

As they approached the outcropping, Arjun noticed an unusual formation in the snow. Years of mountain warfare training had taught him to distinguish between natural patterns and those created by human activity, regardless of how old.

"Hold position," he commanded, raising his fist. His two subordinates instantly froze.

Using his ice axe, Arjun carefully probed the area, alert for any sign of danger. What he initially thought might be a camouflaged explosive or a hidden cache revealed itself to be something entirely unexpected—fabric, preserved in the perpetual ice, protruding slightly from the mountainside where recent avalanche activity had shifted the snowpack.

"Lieutenant, secure the perimeter. Rohit, assist me here."

Working methodically, they excavated what soon became unmistakably human remains—a soldier, his uniform still identifiable despite decades of exposure to the elements. The extreme cold had preserved much of the body and equipment.

"Indian Army, sir," Rohit said quietly, brushing snow from a shoulder patch. "Looks like 1962 pattern."

The Sino-Indian War. The infamous conflict where hundreds of Indian soldiers had disappeared in these mountains, never to return home.

Arjun carefully checked for identification, finding a metal name tag with "Havaldar Randhir Singh, 4th Infantry" still legible. The non-commissioned officer's body was curled protectively around a metal ammunition box, clasped to his chest as if it contained something far more precious than bullets.

With reverent care, Arjun prized the box from the frozen grip. Inside, protected from the elements, lay a carefully folded letter addressed to someone named Leela, alongside a black and white photograph of a young woman wearing a traditional silver anklet.

As Arjun read the letter, written in beautiful Punjabi script, something shifted inside him. The words, penned by a man who knew he might not return, spoke of a love so powerful it transcended the certainty of death. The final paragraphs particularly struck him:

"My dearest Leela,

If this letter reaches you, know that my last thoughts were of your smile during the monsoon dance, when the rain fell upon your silver anklet and created music more beautiful than any I have heard in this life.

If I do not return, please live fully, knowing that what we shared in our brief time together was more precious than what most experience in a lifetime.

Your's Randhir."

Arjun discovered the tears freezing on his cheeks almost instantly in the bitter cold. The raw emotion in those words, written by a man facing his death over sixty years ago, touched something profound within him. In his fifteen years of military service, he had witnessed both the worst and best of humanity, but this; this was something else entirely.

Back at base camp, Colonel Sharma reviewed their findings with typical efficiency.

"Good work recovering the remains, Captain. We'll arrange for proper military transport back to headquarters. The family will be notified if we can locate any surviving relatives."

"Sir," Arjun said, standing at attention in the colonel's office, "I'd like to request two weeks' leave, effective immediately."

Colonel Sharma looked up, surprised. Captain Mehra had never requested unscheduled leave in all his years under the colonel's command.

"May I ask the reason?"

Arjun placed the photograph and letter on the desk. "I want to find her, sir. She deserves to know what happened to him."

The colonel studied his officer's face, recognizing the determination in his eyes.

"This is highly unusual, Captain. She may not even be alive."

"With respect, sir, it's something I need to do." Arjun paused. "Some stories deserve an ending."

Colonel Sharma considered him for a long moment before nodding. "Two weeks, Captain. I'll arrange for the paperwork."

As Arjun left the office, the weathered photograph of Leela tucked carefully in his breast pocket, he couldn't explain, even to himself, why finding this woman had suddenly become so important to him. Perhaps it was the isolation of his own life, devoted entirely to service with little room for personal connections. or perhaps it was simply that some stories, once encountered, demands to be completed.

Whatever the reason, as the transport helicopter lifted him away from the mountain base the next morning, Arjun felt a sense of purpose different from any mission he had undertaken before. Havaldar Randhir Singh and his beloved Leela had waited sixty-three years to be reunited. Their story would not remain unfinished any longer.

2

Monsoon Hearts

The summer of 1960 brought change to the small village near Amritsar. The wheat fields stretched golden to the horizon, rippling in gentle waves under the June sun as nineteen-year-old Randhir Singh worked alongside his father. The calluses on his hands had formed years ago, hardened from endless days of agricultural labour, yet he took pride in the work that sustained his family through generations.

"A new school teacher arrives today," his father mentioned, pausing to wipe sweat from his brow. "From Delhi, they say a university man."

Randhir nodded absently, more concerned with finishing the harvest before the predicted evening rains. Education meant little to most families in their village, where boys typically completed basic schooling before committing fully to family fields or trades. Randhir himself had been an exception, studying until sixteen before duty called him back to the land.

Later that afternoon, as he led their ox-drawn cart through the village center, he noticed the commotion outside the small schoolhouse. A tired-looking Ambassador car with Delhi plates had attracted a crowd of curious onlookers, mostly children who rarely saw vehicles from the capital.

From the passenger side emerged a girl who immediately captured Randhir's attention. She wore a simple cotton salwar kameez, but carried herself with an unmistakable city grace. Her hair, braided and falling to her waist, caught the sunlight as she turned to help an older man; presumably her father with their luggage.

Without intending to, Randhir found himself slowing the cart.

"Welcome, welcome!" The village headman approached the newcomers. "Mohan Sharma ji, we are honored by your arrival. The children have been without proper instruction since our previous teacher's passing."

The man smiled tiredly. "Thank you for the welcome. This is my daughter, Leela. She has come to assist me while continuing her own studies."

As if sensing his gaze, the girl looked up, meeting Randhir's eyes across the dusty square. The moment stretched between them, until his ox, impatient with the delay, lurched forward, breaking the connection.

That night, during dinner with his parents and younger siblings, Randhir found himself unusually quiet.

"You saw the new teacher's daughter," his mother stated rather than asked, her keen eyes missing nothing. "She's pretty, they say."

"I wouldn't know," Randhir mumbled, focusing on his food.

His father snorted. "The Sharma's are Brahmins from Delhi. Their daughter will marry a city boy with education, not a farmer. Don't waste your thoughts there, son."

Randhir nodded in agreement, yet the brief connection he'd felt remained stubbornly in his mind.

In the weeks that followed, the village adapted to the new schoolteacher and his daughter. Mohan Sharma proved to be passionate about education, while Leela started a small reading circle for the village girls who rarely attended formal classes beyond basic literacy.

Their paths crossed occasionally, at the village well, in the small market, or during community gatherings. Each time, Randhir felt the same inexplicable pull, though propriety and social barriers kept their interactions brief and formal.

Everything changed during the festival of Baisakhi in April 1961. The entire village gathered to celebrate the harvest with music, dancing, and feasting. Colourful decorations transformed the village square, and even the most conservative elders relaxed their usual restrictions.

Randhir, having recently returned from a two-week training camp with the territorial army reserves he had joined the previous year, found himself standing near the musicians as Leela performed a traditional Punjabi dance with other young women. Her movements were precise yet fluid, her face alive with joy as she twirled to the rhythm of the dhol.

When the dance ended and the audience dispersed for refreshments, he found himself alone with her for the first time.

"You're the farmer with the stubborn ox," she said, her eyes twinkling with amusement.

Randhir laughed despite himself. "And you're the teacher's daughter who started a revolution among our women."

"Is education revolutionary?" she challenged.

"In places where tradition is everything? Yes." He hesitated. "I think it's good, what you're doing. My sisters attend your reading circle."

She studied him with sudden interest. "You don't speak like most farmers' sons."

"I read when I can, History mostly." He felt self-conscious under her gaze. "Your father lent me a book about the Mauryan Empire last week."

Their conversation flowed easily after that, discovering shared interests despite their different backgrounds. As the evening progressed, they found themselves walking along the edge of the celebration, voices lowered in passionate discussion about everything from ancient Indian kingdoms to poetry.

"My father would say I'm being too forward," Leela said finally, glancing back toward the lights of the festival.

"My father would say the same about me," Randhir admitted. "Our families wouldn't approve of... friendship between us."

She met his eyes directly. "And what would you say, Randhir Singh?"

"That some things are worth the disapproval."

Their meetings became clandestine after that, brief encounters at the village temple, conversations disguised as chance meetings at the market, notes passed through Randhir's youngest sister who attended Leela's reading circle. Despite the secrecy, those months were filled with a growing connection neither had experienced before.

By the monsoon season of 1961, what had begun as intellectual curiosity had blossomed into something deeper. During a sudden downpour in July, they found shelter in an abandoned storage shed on the outskirts of the village. With rain drumming against the tin roof, they shared their first kiss, tentative and sweet, breaking barriers of caste and custom that had stood for generations.

"I'll leave for military training next month," Randhir told her, their foreheads pressed together. "Three months at the infantry school."

"Will you return to farming after?"

"No," he admitted. "I've enlisted properly in the regular army 4 years, at least."

Her eyes widened. "You didn't tell me."

"I was afraid to." He took her hands in his. "I'll be stationed near the Chinese border after training. The situation there is... uncertain."

"You're afraid I won't wait," she whispered.

"I'm afraid I'm asking too much. Your father wants you to study in Delhi next year. You could meet someone more suitable"

She silenced him with another kiss. "I choose who is suitable for me, Randhir."

On the night before his departure for training, they met one last time. The village was celebrating the harvest festival, with dancing scheduled in the central square despite the light rain that had been falling all day. Under cover of the festivities, they slipped away to their meeting place.

Randhir carried a small package wrapped in silk.

"I wanted to give you something," he said, suddenly nervous. "To remember our promise."

Inside the package laid a delicate silver anklet, simple but beautifully crafted, with tiny bells that made the softest music when moved.

"It was my grandmother's," he explained. "The only valuable thing I own."

Leela's eyes filled with tears as she allowed him to fasten it around her ankle. She moved her foot slightly, making the bells chime.

"Like the rain on the roof that day," she whispered.

They danced together in their private shelter, the anklet creating gentle music with each step, a memory they would each carry through the difficult times ahead.

"When I return," Randhir promised, "I'll speak to your father properly. No more secrets."

"And if he refuses?"

"Then we'll find another way. But I'll come back to you, Leela. Whatever happens."

Two days later, he boarded the train for his infantry training, the image of Leela standing in the rain, her silver anklet catching the last light of dusk, burned into his memory.

Neither could have known that tensions with China would escalate dramatically in the coming months, nor that their promises would soon be tested in ways they couldn't imagine.

3

The Final Battle

(October 1962)

The military outpost near Ladakh sat like a fragile human assertion against the overwhelming dominance of the mountains. Havaldar Randhir Singh pulled his standard-issue coat tighter against the biting October wind as he completed his perimeter check. After fifteen months of regular army service, eleven of them at this remote posting, he had learned to read the mountains' moods like a language and tonight they seemed restless, warning of something beyond the usual winter preparations.

"Tea, Randhir?" Havaldar Suraj Kumar approached, carrying two steaming cups.

As the only other Punjabi speaker in their unit, Suraj had become Randhir's closest friend during these long months of border duty.

"Thanks." Randhir accepted the cup gratefully, the heat seeping through his gloves.

They stood in companionable silence, watching the sunset paint the snow-capped peaks in shades of fire before fading to purple shadow. Below their position, the valley sprawled in deepening darkness.

"Mail came while you were on patrol," Suraj said finally. "There's one from your school teacher girl."

Despite the cold, Randhir felt warmth spread through him. Leela's letters, arriving irregularly due to their remote location, had become his lifeline during this deployment. Each one was read repeatedly until the paper became soft and the ink began to fade.

"And the newspapers?" he asked.

Suraj's expression sobered. "More of the same. The Chinese are calling our forward positions 'aggressive incursions.' Delhi says we're only defending our territory."

"What do you think?"

"I think," Suraj said carefully, "that we're thirty-two men with World War II era rifles, holding a position that both governments have suddenly decided is strategically crucial."

They'd had this conversation many times in recent weeks. The tension between India and China had been escalating steadily, with diplomatic communications breaking down and military postings increasing on both sides.

"The reinforcements must arrive soon," Randhir said, more to reassure himself than because he had believed it. Their promised relief and supply column was now two weeks overdue.

Back in their tiny barracks, Randhir unfolded Leela's letter by lamplight. Her elegant script covered three pages, describing her university courses in Delhi, her mother's illness that had delayed her studies for a semester and the letters from Randhir's younger sisters who faithfully reported village news.

"Your father stopped me temple last month," she wrote. "He asked when you would return on leave. I think he suspects something, but there was no anger in his question only a father's concern. Perhaps our fears of family opposition were exaggerated? When you return, I believe we may find more understanding than we anticipated."

Randhir traced his fingers over her signature. The possibility that their families might accept their relationship seemed almost too much to hope for, yet Leela's optimism was contagious even across hundreds of kilometers.

The letter's final paragraph grasped his heart:

"I wear your grandmother's anklet every day, though hidden beneath my salwar. When I walk alone in the evenings, I deliberately step harder to hear its music and feel you walking beside me. Come back to me, my love. The monsoons have passed without you for too long."

Folding the letter carefully, Randhir reached for paper to write his reply. He had begun a routine of writing to Leela whenever he received her letters, pouring his heart onto pages that might take weeks to reach her. Tonight, however, something held him back; uneasiness he couldn't name.

Instead of the usual updates about his daily duties and reassurances of his affection, he found himself writing something different:

"My dearest Leela,

The mountains are restless tonight. In the fifteen months I've served at this outpost, I've come to understand that these ancient peaks have their own wisdom. They know what approaches before any human sentinel can detect it.

There are rumours among the men that the Chinese forces have been moving equipment and troops to positions just beyond our observation points. Our commanding officer dismisses these as imagination, but many of us feel that something significant is building.

I do not write this to worry you, but because I find myself thinking more than usual about what matters most in life. If my time in the army has taught me anything, it is that we must not leave important words unspoken."

His pen hesitated over the paper before continuing:

"I have never told you about the night before I left for training, when we danced in the rain and you wore my grandmother's anklet for the first time. That moment with the sound of water on the roof and the tiny bells around your ankle creating our own private music was when I knew with absolute certainty that you are the great love of my life.

Whatever happens in the coming days or years, please know that loving you has made me a better man than I would have been without you. Your belief in me gave me courage to reach beyond what was expected, to see possibilities I never would have considered."

Randhir continued writing until the lamp began to sputter, filling page after page with memories of their time together and hopes for their future. He wrote as if these might be the last words she would ever receive from him, though he tried to dismiss such thoughts as mere superstition.

In the final paragraphs, he allowed himself to dream on paper:

"When my service concludes next year, I will return not to my father's fields but to you. With my army savings, we can begin a small business in Amritsar—perhaps the bookshop we've discussed, where you can continue your studies while I manage the accounts. Your father, the dedicated teacher, might even approve of a son-in-law who values education enough to build a life around it.

My dearest Leela, if this letter reaches you, know that my last thoughts were of your smile during the monsoon dance, when the rain fell upon your silver anklet and created music more beautiful than any I have heard in this life. I go to face whatever comes with the memory of your love giving me courage.

If I do not return, please live fully, knowing that what we shared in our brief time together was more precious than what most experience in a lifetime.

Your's Randhir"

Reading over what he had written, Randhir felt a momentary embarrassment at the letter's somber tone. There was no concrete reason to believe he faced immediate danger. Yet something prevented him from rewriting it in a more optimistic voice.

He sealed the letter in an envelope along with a small pressed flower he had collected during a patrol, and then placed it in the metal ammunition box where he kept his personal items.

Just before dawn on October 20, 1962, the sentry's urgent shout roused the outpost. Through his binoculars, Randhir observed what they had feared for weeks; Chinese troops advancing in force toward their position, with artillery support visible in the distance.

"Radio the headquarters," their commanding officer ordered his voice steady despite the obvious gravity of the situation.

The communications officer emerged from the radio room minutes later, his face grim. "No response, sir. The frequencies are being jammed."

What followed was a desperate scramble to prepare defences, it was never meant to withstand a serious assault. By mid-morning, the first artillery shells began to fall around their position.

"They'll overrun us within hours," Suraj said quietly as they took cover behind a stone wall, his normally cheerful face now solemn. "We need to get a message through to headquarters."

Their commanding officer reached the same conclusion. "We need volunteers for a messenger mission," he announced. "It's critical that command knows the scale of this attack and our position."

Randhir and Suraj exchanged a look before stepping forward simultaneously. They were assigned to different routes; Suraj heading southwest toward the nearest Indian outpost, while Randhir would attempt a more dangerous eastern path that might bypass the advancing forces.

Before departing, Randhir retrieved the metal box containing his letter to Leela and a few personal effects.

"If you make it through and I don't," he told Suraj, "find me and make sure she gets this."

Suraj clasped his friend's shoulder. "We'll laugh about this conversation over chai in Delhi next month."

But his eyes, solemn and knowing, told a different story.

They departed as artillery fire intensified. Randhir's route took him through a narrow mountain pass where loose stones made silent movement impossible. As Chinese mortar fire began targeting the area, he took refuge in a small cave, planning to continue after nightfall.

The daylight hours passed in tense waiting, punctuated by distant explosions and gunfire from the direction of the outpost. As dusk approached, Randhir prepared to resume his journey when he heard voices; Chinese soldiers establishing a position directly in his path.

In the gathering darkness, he attempted to backtrack toward a different route, only to encounter another patrol. What followed was a desperate game of evasion through increasingly treacherous terrain as night fell completely.

Forced higher into the mountains to avoid detection, Randhir found himself navigating narrow ledges in near-total darkness. The metal box containing his letter to Leela was secured inside his coat, close to his heart, as he inched along a precipitous drop.

A sudden explosion from the valley below; larger than the previous artillery fire, illuminated the mountainside momentarily. In that flash of light, Randhir saw Chinese soldiers on the path ahead, cutting off his escape route.

His options exhausted, he made a final desperate attempt to scale a near-vertical face that might lead to a path beyond their position. As he climbed, loose rocks gave way beneath his boots. The fall was silent except for his single, sharp intake of breath as he plummeted into darkness.

The official report, compiled weeks later after the ceasefire, listed Havaldar Randhir Singh among thirty-eight soldiers missing in action, presumed dead. The report noted that the outpost had been completely overrun, with only seven survivors, including Havaldar Suraj Kumar, who had successfully delivered news of the attack despite serious injuries.

What the report didn't mention was Suraj's return to the region after recovering from his wounds, his private mission to find any trace of his friend despite the military's prohibition against unauthorized searches. Nor did it record his eventual reluctant conclusion that Randhir must have perished somewhere in the vast, unforgiving mountains that had claimed so many lives during those twenty-one days of conflict.

In a small ammunition box, pressed against the heart of a soldier lost to the mountains, a letter to a waiting lover remained undelivered as snow began to fall, covering all evidence of the battle and beginning sixty-three years of silence.

4

Echoes across Decades

The morning air in Delhi carried the distinct fragrance of early spring; a subtle sweetness beneath the ever-present urban smells of exhaust and spices. Captain Arjun Mehra barely noticed as he climbed the worn steps of the National Archives building, his mind focused entirely on the task ahead.

Three days had passed since his discovery of Havaldar Randhir Singh's remains, and Arjun had used every moment to prepare for this search. The military records division had provided basic information: Randhir Singh had enlisted in 1961, served with distinction in the 4th Infantry Division, and was reported missing in action during the Sino-Indian War of 1962. His home village was listed as Rattangarh near

Amritsar, and his next of kin at time of enlistment was his father, Gurnam Singh.

What the official records didn't mention; not even once was anyone named Leela.

"May I help you, Captain?" The archivist, a thin man with wire-rimmed glasses and a government-issued cardigan despite the warming weather, appraised Arjun's uniform with professional interest.

"I'm researching a soldier lost in the '62 conflict," Arjun explained, presenting his military ID and research authorization. "I need access to personnel records, any surviving unit diaries, and civilian correspondence from that period."

The archivist's eyebrows rose. "Civilian correspondence?"

"Letters to and from soldiers on the front," Arjun clarified. "Particularly anything sent to or from Havaldar Randhir Singh of the 4th Infantry."

"Most personal correspondence wouldn't have been preserved," the archivist cautioned. "But I'll see what we have."

Hours melted away as Arjun immersed himself in the fragile documents of a war largely forgotten by the public consciousness. The 1962 conflict had been brief but devastating, with poor equipment, insufficient high-altitude training, and flawed strategic decisions leading to significant Indian casualties.

Randhir's unit records painted a picture of a capable, intelligent soldier who had risen quickly to the rank of Havaldar despite his limited formal education. His commanding officer's notes described him as "unusually thoughtful" and "demonstrates leadership beyond his years"assessments that matched the eloquence and depth of feeling in the letter Arjun had found.

By late afternoon, Arjun had compiled a substantial dossier on Randhir's military service but found no mention of his relationship with Leela. As the archives prepared to close, the archivist approached with a final folder.

"I remembered we have a collection of oral histories from veterans, recorded in the 1990s," he explained. "Two men from the 4th Infantry participated. They might have known your soldier."

Arjun accepted the folder gratefully. "Thank you. This could be invaluable."

"May I ask," The archivist said hesitantly, "why this particular soldier? We lost many men in that conflict."

Arjun considered the question. "I found his remains during a mountain reconnaissance mission. He'd written a letter to someone he loved; a woman named Leela. It never reached her."

The archivist's professional detachment softened. "And you're trying to deliver it sixty years later?"

"Something likes that."

The next morning Arjun found himself in a modest apartment in a Delhi suburb, seated across from retired Colonel Vijay Sharma, one of the veterans who had provided an oral history. At eighty-five, the colonel remained military in his bearing despite his age, his back straight and his white moustache precisely trimmed.

"Randhir Singh," the old soldier repeated eyes distant with memory. "Yes, I remember him. Quiet, thoughtful lad. Always had a book when off duty, which was unusual then. The men called him 'Professor' behind his back, though respectfully."

"Do you recall if he ever mentioned someone named Leela?"

The colonel's weathered face creased in concentration. "Can't say that he did. We didn't discuss personal matters much at that outpost. Conditions were difficult; minimal supplies outdated equipment, constant tensions. But I do remember he wrote letters whenever possible. More than most."

"To his family?"

"Perhaps. Though once..." colonel paused, searching his memory. "Yes, there was an incident. A supply drop brought mail, and he received a letter that transformed him. For days afterward, he seemed to walk above the ground. The men noticed. There was good-natured teasing about a sweetheart back home."

Arjun leaned forward. "Did he ever mention who she was?"

"Not to me. But his friend might know; Suraj Kumar. They were inseparable. Both Punjabi boys, both from farming families. If Randhir confided in anyone, it would have been Suraj."

"Is he still alive?"

"Last I heard, yes. Settled in Chandigarh after retirement. Decorated veteran he got a message through during the Chinese attack that saved many lives, despite being wounded himself."

This information proved crucial. By that evening, Arjun had located a phone number for retired Major Suraj Kumar, but his call went unanswered. Deciding this lead would require a personal visit, he turned his attention to the other veteran from the oral history project.

Former Lance Naik Deepak Rai, now living in a military retirement community in Delhi, had served briefly with Randhir's unit before being transferred. His recollections were less detailed, but he offered one significant insight.

"Singh was different from most soldiers," the elderly man told Arjun, his voice thin but clear. "Had ambitions beyond returning to his village. Talked about opening a bookshop after his service. Unusual for a farmer's son in those days."

A bookshop. The detail resonated with something in Randhir's letter to Leela: With my army savings, we can begin a small business in Amritsar perhaps the bookshop we've discussed.

Arjun's search was beginning to feel less abstract, the historical figures transforming into real people with dreams that had been brutally interrupted.

Two days later, he arrived in Rattangarh, the small village near Amritsar listed as Randhir's home. Little had changed in the rural Punjab landscape since Randhir's time; the same golden wheat fields stretched to the horizon, though now punctuated by the occasional cell phone towers or satellite dishes.

The village itself had grown somewhat, with concrete structures intermixed with traditional buildings, but it retained the essential character of an agricultural community. At the small tea shop in the village center, Arjun's uniform drew curious glances.

"I'm looking for information about a soldier from this village," he explained to the proprietor, an elderly man with a full white beard. "Havaldar Randhir Singh, son of Gurnam Singh. He went missing in the 1962 war."

The name created an immediate stir among the older patrons. One man, his face deeply creased from decades of working under the Punjab sun, approached slowly.

"You speak of Gurnam Singh's eldest son? The one lost in the mountains?"

Arjun nodded. "Yes. We've found his remains."

A reverent silence fell over the shop. The old man touched his forehead in respect.

"After all these years," he murmured. "Gurnam died still waiting for news of his boy. The family is gone now; the younger son sold the land and moved to Canada many years ago. But those of us who remember, we still speak of Randhir. He brought honour to our village."

"Did he have... a sweetheart here?" Arjun asked carefully. "Someone named Leela?"

The question caused an exchange of glances among the elders. The old man who had first spoken nodded slowly.

"The schoolteacher's daughter. They thought no one knew, but in a village like this..." He smiled sadly. "Their secret was no secret at all."

Another elder added, "A forbidden match in those days; different castes, different worlds. But they were young and in love. After news came that Randhir was missing, the teacher took his family away. No one in the village blamed him. His daughter was... devastated."

"Do you know where they went?"

"The father was from Pathankot originally. They returned there, I believe. The man's name was Mohan Sharma; a respected teacher."

With each new piece of information, Leela and Randhir became more real to Arjun. Their story, young love defying social conventions, separated by war; affected him more deeply than he had anticipated.

What had begun as a mission of military duty
was evolving into something more personal.

Before leaving Rattangarh, Arjun visited the site
where Randhir's family home had once stood.
The current owner, learning of his purpose,
respectfully showed him the property, including
an ancient banyan tree where, according to
village lore, young couples had met secretly for
generations.

"They say Randhir and the city girl would meet
here," the man told him. "My grandmother used
to tell how the girl wore a silver anklet that made
music when she walked."

Standing under the spreading branches of the
tree that had witnessed their love story, Arjun
felt an unexpected connection to the young
soldier whose remains he had discovered. They
had both chosen military service, both
understood the isolation it often brought. But
Randhir had found something Arjun had never

prioritized in his own life; a love worth remembering for sixty years.

As he departed Rattangarh, Arjun found himself wondering about Leela, the young woman in the photograph with intelligent eyes and a gentle smile. Had she waited for Randhir? Had she eventually found happiness elsewhere? The letter in Randhir's possession had urged her to live fully if he didn't return, showing a selflessness that impressed Arjun deeply.

His next destination was Pathankot, where he hoped to pick up the trail of Mohan Sharma and his daughter Leela. What had been a simple delivery mission was becoming a journey through time, tracing the ripples of a love story that had persisted in memory long after its protagonists had disappeared from the village where it began.

As the train carried him across the Punjab countryside, Arjun reflected on the peculiar nature of his quest. In fifteen years of military service, he had never imagined himself as a messenger for a love story decades old. Yet something about Randhir and Leela's interrupted relationship resonated within him, creating an urgency that went beyond professional duty.

Perhaps it was the recognition of his own solitary existence; a life defined by service but lacking the deep personal connections that had given Randhir's short life such meaning. Or perhaps it was simply that some stories, once encountered, demanded completion.

5

Paths She Took

Pathankot greeted Arjun with the chaotic energy typical of Punjab's smaller cities—a cacophony of auto-rickshaws, street vendors, and the persistent honking that formed the soundtrack of urban India. The spring heat had settled fully now, and he wiped perspiration from his brow as he navigated from the railway station to the city's education department.

"Government Higher Secondary School," the clerk confirmed after checking decades-old records. "Mohan Sharma taught English and History there from late 1962 to 1965. Yes, he had previously been posted to a village school near Amritsar."

"And his daughter?" Arjun prompted.

The clerk shrugged. "Family details wouldn't be in these records, sir. But the school still exists. Someone there might remember."

The school building, constructed during the British colonial era, stood with dignified fatigue at the end of a tree-lined avenue. Classes were in session, children's voices drifting through open windows as Arjun was escorted to the principal's office.

The current principal, a woman in her fifties, listened to his inquiry with growing interest. "Mohan Sharma is before my time, but our retired vice-principal might remember. He's been associated with this institution for over fifty years."

A phone call later, arrangements were made to meet Kailash Bhatia, the former vice-principal, at his home that afternoon.

"Mohan Sharma," the elderly educator mused when Arjun explained his mission. They sat in Bhatia's small garden, where carefully tended roses provided respite from the urban surroundings. "Yes, I was a young teacher when he joined our staff. Brilliant mind, dedicated educator. He came here rather suddenly from a village posting, as I recall."

"With his daughter?"

"Leela, yes." Bhatia's face softened with recollection. "Extraordinary young woman. She had been admitted to Delhi University before they moved here, but deferred her studies to accompany her father. There was talk that she was recovering from some personal tragedy."

"Did she ever mention someone named Randhir Singh?"

The old teacher's eyes sharpened with sudden recognition. " The soldier, of course. She never spoke of him directly, but the story circulated among the staff. Mohan confided in our principal that his daughter was in mourning for a young man reported missing in the Chinese conflict." He paused, his expression somber. "She was...not well when they first arrived. Refused to eat, rarely spoke. Her father was deeply concerned."

"How long did they stay in Pathankot?"

"About three years. Then Mohan accepted a position at a prestigious school in Shimla. The mountain air, he said, might help Leela recover her spirits." Bhatia hesitated. "Before they left, she had begun assisting in our library. Books seemed to provide her only comfort."

A bookshop, Arjun thought. Another connection to the dreams Randhir had described in his letter.

"Do you know where in Shimla they went?"

"Auckland House School, if I'm not mistaken. It was considered a step up professionally for Mohan."

With each conversation, each new detail, Arjun felt increasingly invested in Leela's story. The photograph he carried; showing a vibrant young woman with bright eyes,contrasted sharply with the grieving, silent figure described by Bhatia. What must it have been like for her, waiting for news that never came, hope gradually giving way to despair?

The next morning found him on another train, this one climbing steadily into the foothills of the Himalayas toward Shimla. The former summer capital of British India retained much of its colonial architecture, buildings clinging to the mountainsides like artifacts from another era.

At Auckland House School, the registrar confirmed that Mohan Sharma had indeed taught there from 1965 to 1970. "His daughter worked in the administration office while completing her degree through correspondence," she added, consulting ancient ledgers. "They lived in the faculty quarters on campus."

"Would anyone still remember them?"

The registrar hesitated. "Most from that era have passed on. But Dr. Verma might recall them—he was a young biology teacher then, before he left for his medical studies."

Dr. Aditya Verma, now in his eighties and long retired from his medical practice, received Arjun in his hillside home with the courteous formality of his generation. When Arjun explained his search, the elderly physician's expression grew thoughtful.

"Leela Sharma," he said quietly. "Yes, I remember her well. Beautiful, intelligent, but carrying a profound sadness. I was completing my final year of teaching before medical school when they arrived."

"Did you know her well?"

"Not initially. She kept to herself." Dr. Verma poured tea with precise movements. "But as the school physician's assistant, I encountered her when she experienced what we would now recognize as panic attacks. Her father brought her to the infirmary several times."

Arjun leaned forward. "She was still suffering from her loss."

"Profoundly so. In confidence, her father shared that she had been engaged to marry a soldier lost in the '62 conflict. Not formally engaged; the families hadn't approved, but they had pledged themselves to each other."

"Did she ever recover?"

Dr. Verma's expression softened. "Grief changes shape, Captain. It doesn't vanish. But yes, gradually she began to reengage with life. By my final year at the school, before I left for medical college in Delhi, she had regained some measure of peace." He paused, seeming to recall something specific. "She wore an silver anklet, with small bells. I noticed because she would sometimes touch it absently when lost in thought."

The anklet. Arjun felt a surge of emotion at this confirmation that Leela had kept this tangible connection to Randhir.

"Do you know what happened to her after you left?"

"Our paths crossed again years later, quite by chance. I had established my practice in Delhi, and she came in as a patient." Dr. Verma smiled at the memory.

"I hardly recognized her at first. She had married by then; a colleague of mine, actually. Dr. Rajiv Kapoor, a respected psychiatrist. They had two children."

Arjun absorbed this information with mixed feelings. He was glad that Leela had eventually found happiness, just as Randhir had wished for her in his final letter. Yet he couldn't help feeling a touch of melancholy that their love story had never reached its intended conclusion.

"Do you know if she's still alive? I would like to deliver Randhir's last letter to her."

The doctor's face fell. "I'm afraid she passed away about three years ago. Cancer, I believe. Dr. Kapoor preceded her in death by several years."

A heavy silence filled the room. After coming so far, following Leela's path across decades, Arjun felt the sharp sting of disappointment. He had been too late.

"She had children, you said?"

"Yes, a daughter and son. The daughter; Priya, I believe, was a doctor like her parents. The son went abroad, America perhaps."

"Would you happen to know where they lived in Delhi?"

"East Delhi, I believe. Priya continued to practice at the same hospital where her parents had worked; All India Institute of Medical Sciences. You might inquire there."

Three days later, Arjun stood before a well-maintained two-story house in a quiet East Delhi neighbourhood. The garden showed signs of careful attention, with spring flowers adding colour to the otherwise modest exterior.

He hesitated before pressing the doorbell, suddenly uncertain about intruding on a family's grief with news of a love that had preceded their existence. How would Leela's children feel about this ghost from their mother's past?

Before he could reconsider, the door opened to reveal a woman in her late fourty, with streaks of few grey in her dark hair and eyes that immediately reminded Arjun of the photograph he carried—Leela's eyes, looking at him across generations.

"Dr. Priya Kapoor?" he asked.

"Yes?" She regarded his uniform with polite curiosity.

"My name is Captain Arjun Mehra. I've come about your mother; and about a man named Randhir Singh."

Something flickered in her expression recognition, not surprise. Without a word, she stepped aside to allow him entry, leading him into a sitting room where bookshelves lined the walls. Arjun noticed a medical degree displayed alongside family photographs; including one of an elderly woman whose smile he recognized from a sixty-year-old photograph.

"You've found him, haven't you?" Priya asked quietly, her composed demeanour suggesting she had been waiting for this moment. "After all these years."

6

Learning to Live

(November 1962)

The telegram arrived on a Tuesday. Leela was helping her mother prepare lunch when the messenger arrived at their quarters in the village school compound. She watched through the window as her father signed for the envelope, his expression changing as he read its contents.

When he entered the kitchen, his face told her everything before he spoke a word.

"Randhir Singh has been reported missing in action," he said gently. "During the Chinese offensive last month."

Her mother gasped, reaching for Leela, but she remained perfectly still, as if movement might make the news real.

"Missing," she finally said. "Not confirmed dead."

Her father's eyes held compassion. "Leela;"

"Missing means they haven't found him," she insisted, her voice rising. "It means he could still be alive, waiting for rescue, or injured, or..."

"The entire outpost was overrun," her father explained softly. "Only a few survived. They've searched, beta."

The walls seemed to close in around her. The silver anklet felt suddenly heavy against her skin as she backed away from her parents, shaking her head in denial.

"No," she whispered. "He promised he would come back."

That night began what her parents would later call "the silence"months during which Leela spoke only when absolutely necessary, moving through each day like an automation. She stopped attending her university correspondence courses, stopped reading the books that had once given her such pleasure, stopped everything except the mechanical process of survival.

In February 1963, four months after the telegram arrived, her father made a decision.

"I've accepted a teaching position in Pathankot," he announced over dinner. "We'll leave at the end of the school term."

Leela looked up from her barely touched food. "I can't leave," she said, breaking her longest stretch of silence. "What if he comes back and can't find me?"

Her father reached across the table to take her hand. "Beta, you know in your heart...."

"You don't understand," she interrupted, her voice cracking with emotion. "We had a promise. I need to be here."

"Leela," her mother said gently, "Randhir would not want you to stop living. You know this."

Later that night, alone in her room, Leela removed the silver anklet for the first time since Randhir had placed it on her ankle. She held it to the lamplight, watching the tiny bells catch the glow.

"Where are you?" she whispered. "I feel you're still alive. Somewhere."

Despite her protests, the family relocated to Pathankot in June 1963. The larger city offered little comfort to Leela, who withdrew further into herself. Concerned about her declining health, her father arranged for her to see a doctor, who diagnosed "acute melancholia" and prescribed rest and sedatives; remedies that addressed symptoms but not the devastation at their core.

On the anniversary of Randhir's disappearance, Leela locked herself in her room with pen and paper. For hours, she wrote, everything she would have told him over the past year, every thought, every feeling, every moment she had wished to share. When finished, she carefully folded the pages and placed them in a wooden box alongside his few letters and the photograph of them together that her youngest sister had secretly taken during the harvest festival.

This became her annual ritual; a day spent writing to Randhir as if he might somehow receive her words, as if the connection between them remained unbroken despite all evidence to the contrary.

In the summer of 1964, under pressure from her increasingly worried parents, Leela agreed to volunteer at the school library. Among the books, she found a measure of peace that had eluded her elsewhere. The quiet order of the stacks, the familiar scent of paper and binding glue, reminded her of discussions with Randhir about the bookshop they had planned to open together.

"You would have loved this," she whispered one afternoon, running her fingers along leather-bound classics. "Perhaps I can build our dream for both of us."

By 1965, when her father accepted the position in Shimla, Leela had regained some outward semblance of normalcy. She resumed her studies through correspondence courses, focusing on literature and education. To casual observers, she appeared to be recovering from her grief.

Only her parents understood that she had not moved beyond her loss but had instead built a life around it; a life that accommodated her on-going connection to Randhir while allowing her to function in the world.

In Shimla, the family settled into faculty housing at Auckland House School. The mountain setting provided a fresh start, with the colonial architecture and pine-scented air creating an environment far removed from the Punjab village where her heart had been broken.

It was in Shimla, during a panic attack that left her struggling to breathe, that Leela first encountered young Dr. Aditya Verma, the school's assistant physician.

"Focus on my voice," he instructed calmly, as she gasped for air in the school infirmary. "Count with me: one, two, and three..."

When the attack subsided, embarrassment replaced fear. "I'm sorry," she mumbled. "This happens sometimes."

"No apology needed," he replied. "The mind and body remember what we try to forget."

Something in his matter-of-fact acceptance prompted her to add, "My fiancé was lost in the war with China. Not officially my fiancé; we never had that chance."

Dr. Verma didn't offer platitudes or awkward sympathy. Instead, he simply nodded and said, "That's a heavy burden to carry alone."

Over the following months, Leela found herself seeking out Dr. Verma's company during his library visits. Their conversations, initially focused on books, gradually expanded to include personal confidences. He spoke of his ambition to become a psychiatrist, his fascination with the human mind's response to trauma and healing.

"Grief isn't an illness to be cured," he told her once. "It's a testimony to love."

When he left for medical school in Delhi in 1966, Leela was surprised by how much she missed their conversations. She had grown accustomed to having someone who allowed her to speak freely of Randhir without judgment or expectation that she should "move on."

The Shimla years brought gradual healing. Leela completed her degree and began teaching literature at a local women's college. Though she maintained her yearly ritual of writing to Randhir on the anniversary of his disappearance, she found herself able to engage more fully with the present.

In the spring of 1968, a letter arrived from Dr. Verma, now completing his residency at All India Institute of Medical Sciences in Delhi. He mentioned that a colleague, Dr. Rajiv Kapoor, was conducting research on grief and memory that might interest her.

"Perhaps you might consider visiting Delhi," he wrote. "The institute is doing ground-breaking work in helping people live with loss rather than merely survive it."

To her parents' surprise and delight, Leela agreed to the visit. Delhi held both painful memories of her interrupted university dreams and the promise of new understanding. During her two-week stay, she attended lectures and support group sessions at Dr. Verma's invitation.

It was where she first met Dr. Rajiv Kapoor; a thoughtful, soft-spoken man, whose work focused on helping families of soldiers missing in action. Unlike many she had encountered, he never suggested that acceptance meant forgetting.

"The relationship doesn't end," he explained during a group session Leela attended. "It transforms. Our challenge is to honour what was while still embracing what is and what might be."

Before returning to Shimla, Leela found herself in a lengthy private conversation with Dr. Kapoor about Randhir. To her surprise, speaking about her lost love to this compassionate stranger proved cathartic rather than painful.

"The silver anklet," Dr. Kapoor noted, glancing at her ankle where the ornament remained partially visible beneath her sari. "It's a beautiful connection to your past."

"I've never taken it off," she admitted. "Not permanently."

"And you shouldn't," he replied simply. "Not unless you choose to."

Over the next two years, Leela maintained correspondence with both Dr. Verma and Dr. Kapoor. When a teaching position opened at a college near Delhi in 1970, she applied and was accepted. Her parents, seeing her growing independence and stability, supported the move though it meant leaving them in Shimla.

In Delhi, Leela continued to participate in Dr. Kapoor's research and support groups, eventually assisting with his work. Their professional relationship gradually evolved into friendship, and then, tentatively, into something deeper.

On a rainy evening reminiscent of another rainy night long ago, Dr. Kapoor asked Leela to join him for dinner at his home. After the meal, seated in his book-lined study, he spoke with characteristic gentleness.

"I have come to care for you deeply, Leela," he said. "I know your heart will always hold Randhir, and I would never ask you to change that. But if you could find room for me as well, I would be honored to share your life."

Leela touched the silver anklet beneath her sari, feeling the familiar weight against her skin. "Rajiv, I don't know if I can....."

"You don't need to answer now," he interrupted softly. "Or ever, if you're not certain. I just wanted you to know."

That night, in her small apartment, Leela took out the wooden box containing her letters to Randhir and the few mementos of their time together. For hours, she sat cross-legged on her bed, reading her own words chronicling seven years of grief, healing, and gradual reengagement with life.

In the most recent letter, written just months earlier, she had described meeting Rajiv, confessing her confusion and guilt at finding herself drawn to his quiet strength and compassion.

"Would you forgive me for feeling this way?" she had written. "Would you understand that loving him doesn't diminish what we shared?"

As dawn broke over Delhi, Leela made her decision. Two months later, she married Dr. Rajiv Kapoor in a simple ceremony attended by both families. Her father, in his toast, spoke of resilience and new beginnings. Her mother wept with relief and happiness.

Only Leela knew that beneath her wedding sari, the silver anklet remained; not as a barrier to her new life, but as an honored part of the journey that had brought her to this moment.

7

Lived in Two Hearts

The Kapoor residence on Lodhi Road quickly became known for its Sunday open houses; gatherings where students, colleagues, and friends would drop by for intellectual discussion, good food, and the warm hospitality that characterized Leela and Rajiv's partnership. Their home, modest but filled with books and art collected during their travels, reflected the harmonious blending of two thoughtful lives.

In the spring of 1972, their family expanded with the birth of their daughter, Priya. Watching Rajiv cradle their new-born with reverent tenderness, Leela felt a fullness of heart she had once thought impossible.

"She has your eyes," Rajiv observed, gazing at their daughter.

"And your contemplative expression," Leela replied, stroking the infant's cheek.

Later that night, after Rajiv had fallen asleep, Leela carefully extracted herself from bed and moved to the small writing desk in the corner of their bedroom. There, by lamplight, she wrote her annual letter to Randhir.

"We have a daughter," she wrote. "When I look at her, I sometimes wonder what our children might have looked like. Would they have had your quiet strength, your thoughtful gaze? I hope you would be happy for me, for this life I've built that honours what we shared while allowing me to move forward. Rajiv understands about you; understands that you occupy a chamber of my heart that remains yours alone."

This bifurcation of her heart became the foundation of her marriage, not a secret kept from her husband, but an honest acknowledgment of her past that Rajiv accepted with extraordinary grace. He never asked her to remove the silver anklet, never showed jealousy of the day each October when she would withdraw to write her letter to Randhir.

In 1975, their son Vikram was born, completing their family. As the children grew, Leela found herself telling them carefully curated stories about "a soldier friend" she had known in her youth. She described his love of books, his dreams of opening a bookshop, his courage in serving his country; building a presence for Randhir in their lives without revealing the full depth of what he had meant to her.

Professionally, the Kapoor's flourished. Rajiv became a leading authority on trauma and grief, while Leela established a respected career teaching literature at Delhi University, eventually publishing scholarly works on themes of loss and resilience in Indian writing. Together, they pioneered programs supporting families of soldiers missing in action, drawing on both academic research and personal experience.

Their marriage, built on mutual respect and deep understanding, provided a stable foundation for their children's development. Priya inherited her parents' compassion and intellectual curiosity, gravitating toward medicine from an early age. Vikram, more artistic in temperament, showed talent in architecture and design.

Through the decades of family milestones, birthdays, graduations, Vikram's eventual move to America for his architectural career; Leela maintained her annual ritual of writing to Randhir. The letters evolved from expressions of grief to thoughtful reflections on her life's journey, always acknowledging the formative impact of their brief time together.

Rajiv discovered these letters accidentally in 1983, finding the wooden box while searching for important documents during a household emergency. That evening, after the crisis had passed, he approached Leela with characteristic gentleness.

"I found your letters," he said simply. "I didn't read them, but I saw who they were addressed to."

Leela felt momentary panic, then relief at his calm expression. "I should have told you about them."

"You've never hidden your past from me, Leela. These letters are part of who you are." He hesitated before adding, "If writing them helps you, then they're important."

In that moment, Leela's appreciation for her husband's generous spirit deepened immeasurably. "Would you like to read them?"

she offered. "Not all, perhaps, but enough to understand."

Rajiv considered before shaking his head. "They're private conversations between you and Randhir. But thank you for being willing to share them."

As their children grew into adulthood, Leela wondered if she should explain the full story of Randhir, particularly to Priya, who had noticed the silver anklet and occasionally asked about its significance. Leela had always deflected, calling it a family heirloom, uncertain how to explain that before their father, there had been another great love in her life.

The opportunity presented itself unexpectedly during Priya's medical school years, when she was assigned a research project on intergenerational trauma. During a weekend visit home, she mentioned interviewing families of soldiers lost in various conflicts.

"It's fascinating how these losses echo through generations," Priya observed. "Even family members born decades after the event carry its impact somehow."

That evening, after Rajiv had gone to bed, Leela invited her daughter into her study. From a locked drawer, she removed the wooden box containing her letters and the few mementos of her time with Randhir.

"There's something I want to share with you," she said, opening the box. "A story that's part of who I am; and therefore, part of you too."

For hours, mother and daughter sat together as Leela finally shared the complete story of her first love, the village romance, the secret meetings, the silver anklet, and the devastating loss that had shaped her early adulthood.

"I've written to him every year since he disappeared," Leela explained, showing Priya the stack of letters. "Your father has always known and understood."

Priya, absorbing this revelation about her mother's past, asked thoughtfully, "Do you think he's still alive somewhere?"

"No," Leela admitted. "Not anymore. But for years, I couldn't accept that he was gone without proof. Writing to him became my way of keeping him with me while still moving forward."

"And the anklet?" Priya gestured toward her mother's ankle.

"A promise that I've kept in my own way."

Priya's reaction reflected the compassionate nature she had inherited from both parents. Far from feeling threatened by this previously unknown presence in their family history, she was moved by the story of enduring love and her father's extraordinary acceptance of sharing his wife's heart.

"Dad is remarkable," she said finally. "To understand this so completely."

"We built our marriage on honesty," Leela replied. "Rajiv never asked me to forget Randhir, only to make room for new love alongside the old."

As Priya rose to leave, she hesitated before asking, "Would you mind if I researched what happened to him? As a medical student, I might have access to military medical records."

Leela felt a surge of emotion at her daughter's offer. "I would appreciate that very much."

Priya's subsequent research yielded little new information beyond what Leela already knew; Havaldar Randhir Singh remained officially classified as missing in action, his body never recovered from the mountainous battlefield. Yet the gesture itself; her daughter's willingness to embrace this aspect of her mother's past, reinforced the integrative healing Leela had achieved over decades.

In 2004, Rajiv was diagnosed with Parkinson's disease. As his health gradually declined over the next decade, the roles in their marriage shifted, with Leela becoming his primary caregiver. Throughout his illness, their bond remained undiminished, their evening conversations continuing to reflect the intellectual and emotional connection that had sustained them for fouty-five years.

On a quiet morning in 2015, Rajiv passed away peacefully in their home, Leela and Priya at his bedside. In the days that followed, as colleagues and former students paid their respects, many spoke of the unique partnership the Kapoor's had modeled; a relationship characterized by profound respect and acceptance.

Priya, who had established her own medical practice in Delhi, suggested that Leela move in with her family after Rajiv's death. "We have plenty of room, Mom. The children would love having you there."

But Leela chose to remain in the home she had shared with Rajiv, though she spent frequent weekends with her daughter's family. "This house holds our life together," she explained. "I find comfort in that."

In the years following Rajiv's death, Leela experienced a renewed connection to her past. At seventy-eight, with her professional life behind her and her daily routines no longer structured around Rajiv's care, memories of her youth in Punjab and her brief time with Randhir surfaced with unexpected vividness.

The silver anklet, worn thin from six decades of daily contact with her skin, remained her constant companion. When arthritis made writing difficult, she dictated her annual letter to

Randhir into a small recorder, later transcribing it with Priya's help.

In early 2021, Leela was diagnosed with advanced ovarian cancer. She approached her illness with the same thoughtful acceptance that had characterized her response to life's previous challenges, refusing aggressive treatments that would diminish the quality of her remaining time.

"I've had a full life," she told her concerned children. "Fuller than many get to experience."

As her strength declined, Leela asked Priya to help her organize her personal effects. Together, they sorted through decades of accumulated papers, books, and mementos. When they came to the wooden box containing her letters to Randhir, Leela made a request that surprised her daughter.

"When I'm gone, I'd like you to continue writing to him once a year," she said. "Just for a while. To let him know what's happening with the family."

Priya, deeply moved by this request, agreed without hesitation. "I'll tell him about your grandchildren, about the hospital wing named after you and him."

In October 2022, now confined to bed and aware that her time was growing short, Leela dictated her final letter to Randhir. Her voice, though weakened by illness, maintained the clear articulation that had captivated generations of students.

"My dearest Randhir," she began, as she had for sixty years. "This will be my last letter to you from this side of whatever separates us. The doctors say I have weeks, perhaps a month. I find I'm not afraid.

"Our love story has been unusual, hasn't it? You, forever twenty-one in my memory, and me, now eighty-three with a lifetime of experiences between us. Yet the connection has never diminished.

"I want you to know that I've had a good life; one filled with purpose and joy alongside the inevitable sorrows. Rajiv was an extraordinary partner who understood that loving him didn't require forgetting you. Our children and grandchildren have brought immeasurable happiness.

"The silver anklet you gave me has never left my ankle. Now I've asked Priya to keep it safe, perhaps for her daughter someday. A tangible thread connecting generations.

"If consciousness continues beyond this life, and if it's true that those we love are waiting for us, then I'll see you soon. And if not; if this is truly the end of our story, then know that you have lived on in my heart every day since our last goodbye.

"Until then, or forever, I remain yours in that special chamber of my heart that has always belonged only to you."

Two weeks later, surrounded by her family, Leela Kapoor closed her eyes for the final time. As requested in her will, the silver anklet was removed from her ankle and given to Priya, along with the wooden box containing sixty years of letters, a chronicle of one woman's journey through grief to a life that honored both what was lost and what was found.

In accordance with Hindu tradition, her ashes were scattered in the Ganga. But in a private ceremony attended only by immediate family, Priya placed a small portion in a special urn adorned with silver bells, to be kept in the family's home altar alongside a photograph of a

young woman in a silver anklet, dancing in the
monsoon rain.

8

Keeper of the Flame

"Please, come in," Priya said, leading Arjun into the sitting room. Her practiced composure; developed through decades of delivering both good and devastating news to patients, couldn't entirely conceal her emotional response to his presence.

Arjun settled onto the offered sofa, acutely aware of the significance of this moment. The journey that had begun with his discovery of Randhir's remains was approaching its culmination, connecting across three generations and more than six decades.

"How did you find him?" Priya asked directly, taking a seat across from him.

"During a reconnaissance mission in the Himalayas," Arjun explained. "His remains were preserved in the ice. He was carrying this."

He removed from his bag, the metal ammunition box, now carefully cleaned and preserved by the Army's conservation team. Priya's hands trembled slightly as she accepted it.

"He was holding it against his chest when we found him," Arjun added softly. "It protected the contents."

Priya opened the box with reverent care. Inside lay Randhir's final letter to Leela, the paper remarkably preserved, along with the small dried flower and the photograph of young Leela wearing the silver anklet.

"May I?" Arjun asked, indicating the letter.

Priya nodded, her eyes never leaving the faded photograph of her mother as a young woman.

"*My dearest Leela*," Arjun read aloud, reciting the poignant final paragraphs that had affected him so deeply when he first discovered them. As he spoke Randhir's words about the monsoon dance and the silver anklet, Priya closed her eyes, visibly moved.

When he finished, she remained silent for a moment before speaking.

"My mother wore that anklet every day of her life," she said finally, her voice steady despite the emotion evident in her eyes. "Even during her wedding to my father, even when she gave birth to me and my brother, even when she died."

She rose and gestured for Arjun to follow. They moved through the house to a small room that appeared to serve as a family prayer space. On a simple wooden altar, alongside traditional religious icons and photographs of departed family members, stood a silver-framed portrait of a young soldier in uniform; Randhir Singh, his serious expression softened by intelligent eyes that seemed to look directly at the viewer.

"She kept his photograph here," Priya explained, "alongside my father and grandparents. When I was growing up, I thought he was simply a relative who had died in the war. It wasn't until I was in medical school that she told me the whole story."

Arjun stared at the photograph, struck by the reality that Randhir had been honored in this home for decades, his presence acknowledged and respected even by the man who had married the woman he loved.

"Your father knew?"

"Not only knew, but understood," Priya replied, her voice filled with admiration. "He never asked her to remove the anklet or to stop writing her annual letters to Randhir. He accepted that my mother's heart was large enough to hold both loves."

From a small drawer beneath the altar, Priya withdrew an object wrapped in silk. Carefully unfolding the fabric, she revealed the silver anklet; delicate, thinned by decades of wear, its tiny bells silent now.

"She willed this to me," Priya explained, "with instructions that it should eventually go to my daughter. A legacy passing through generations."

Arjun felt overwhelmed by the tangible connection to the love story that had consumed his thoughts for the past two weeks. "May I?" he asked, extending his hand.

Priya hesitated only briefly before placing the anklet in his palm. The metal felt warm, as if retaining some essence of the woman who had worn it for sixty years. The craftsmanship was simple but beautiful—the kind of heirloom that carried meaning beyond its material value.

"Would you like to see her letters?" Priya asked quietly.

She led him to her study, where a polished wooden box sat on a bookshelf. Opening it revealed dozens of neatly stacked envelopes; each addressed simply to "Randhir" and dated on the anniversary of his disappearance. Six decades of correspondence to a man long presumed dead but never forgotten.

"She wrote to him every year," Priya explained, "chronicling her life, her joys and sorrows, her continuing connection to him despite building a life with my father. In her final years, when writing became difficult, I helped her transcribe them."

Carefully, she removed the topmost letter, dated October 2022. "Her last one, dictated just weeks before she died."

Arjun read the farewell letter with growing emotion, struck by the lifelong devotion it represented. When he finished, he found himself blinking back tears.

"What an extraordinary woman your mother must have been," he said, carefully returning the letter to Priya.

"She was," Priya agreed. "And equally extraordinary was my father's capacity to share her heart without resentment. He understood that my mother's love for Randhir didn't diminish what she felt for him; that the heart expands to accommodate love rather than dividing it."

Sensing his overwhelming emotion, Priya suggested they continue their conversation over tea. In the kitchen, as she prepared the traditional Indian chai, Arjun noticed photographs displaying a family life rich with connection, Priya with her parents at her medical school graduation, holiday celebrations, moments of ordinary joy captured through decades.

"After my mother told me about Randhir," Priya said as they settled at the kitchen table, "I tried researching what happened to him. Military records were incomplete, and most of his contemporaries had already passed away."

"Did she ever know how he died?"

Priya shook her head. "Only that he was reported missing during the Chinese offensive. The uncertainty was perhaps the cruellest part was not knowing his fate, whether he suffered, whether he might somehow had survived."

"From what we discovered," Arjun explained, "it appears he was attempting to deliver crucial intelligence about the attack when he fell from a mountain path. His remains were preserved in the ice, undisturbed for sixty-three years. He was still clutching the ammunition box containing his letter to your mother."

"Was he..." Priya hesitated. "Did he die instantly?"

Arjun recognized the daughter's need to know her mother's first love had not suffered. "The medical examiner believes so, yes. The fall would have been fatal immediately."

Relief visibly washed over Priya's features. "My mother wondered about that often, whether he had been wounded, whether he had called for her. It would comfort her to know it was quick."

They sat in companionable silence for a moment before Priya spoke again. "What happens now? To his remains?"

"As next of kin can't be located, his parents are deceased and his brother emigrated to Canada decades ago, the Army will provide a military funeral with full honours. His name will be added to the memorial for the 1962 war."

Arjun hesitated before adding, "I thought... perhaps you and your family might want to attend. As Leela's representatives."

Priya's eyes filled with tears. "Yes, we would be honored. My daughter is currently studying medicine in Chandigarh but could return for the ceremony. My brother lives in Boston now, but I'm sure he would make the journey."

As their conversation continued, Arjun shared details of his search, the village elders who remembered the young couple, Dr. Verma in

Shimla, the trail that had led him finally to this home in East Delhi. In turn, Priya filled in gaps in her mother's story, painting a fuller picture of the life Leela had built while keeping Randhir's memory alive.

"Captain Mehra," Priya said as their meeting drew to a close, "may I ask why you pursued this so diligently? Finding my mother, delivering this letter, it goes far beyond military duty."

Arjun considered the question carefully. "When I first read Randhir's letter, something about his words moved me deeply. He wrote with such clarity about what matters most in life; love, connection, honour. In my own career, I've been so focused on service that I've never prioritized those things."

He glanced around at the photographs showing Priya's family life. "Seeing the impact of their love story, how it continued to influence lives decades later; has made me reconsider my own choices."

As he prepared to leave, Priya handed him a sealed envelope. "My mother's final letter to Randhir. I'd like it to be placed with his remains when he's laid to rest, if that's permitted."

"I'll make sure it happens," Arjun promised, accepting the letter with appropriate reverence.

At the door, Priya made one last request. "Would you let me know if you discover anything more about his final mission? My mother always believed he died doing something brave and significant. I'd like to confirm that for her, even now."

"I'll see what I can find," Arjun assured her. "Military records from that conflict are often classified, but given the circumstances, exceptions might be possible."

As he departed the Kapoor home, Arjun felt both emotional weight and unexpected lightness. The story he had been piecing together now had greater depth and context, not just a tragic wartime romance but a complex narrative of love that transcended conventional boundaries and expectations.

Leela and Randhir's relationship had evolved from passionate young love to something more profound, a connection that had shaped multiple lives across generations. And at its center, a simple silver anklet that had witnessed a dance in the monsoon rain more than six decades earlier.

9

Classified Courage

The military archives building in South Block presented a formidable bureaucratic challenge, even for an officer of Arjun's rank. Records from the 1962 conflict remained partially classified, particularly those related to intelligence operations and strategic failures that had contributed to India's defeat.

"I need access to mission reports from Havaldar Randhir Singh's unit," Arjun explained to the severe-looking civilian administrator. "October 1962, just before the Chinese offensive."

The administrator peered at him over wire-rimmed glasses. "Those files are restricted, Captain. You'll need clearance from the Intelligence Directorate."

"His remains have been recovered after sixty-three years," Arjun persisted. "We're preparing for a military funeral. Surely historical context for his service is appropriate."

After several hours of bureaucratic navigation and multiple phone calls to Colonel Sharma for authorization, Arjun finally gained access to a small reading room where redacted files from Randhir's unit were provided under supervision.

The documents confirmed what was already known; the outpost had been undermanned and inadequately equipped when Chinese forces attacked in overwhelming numbers. Communications had been compromised, leaving the isolated position without support or reinforcement.

But between the clinical military language and bureaucratic jargon, Arjun detected significant gaps. References to "special assignments" and "sensitive information" appeared in Randhir's service record without elaboration. Something about his final mission remained deliberately obscured.

With this limited information, Arjun requested permission to interview surviving veterans from that conflict. His request, supported by Colonel Sharma's influence, was grudgingly approved with strict parameters, discussions must focus on Randhir personally, not operational details.

The lead Arjun had been most eager to pursue came from Dr. Verma in Shimla, who had mentioned that Randhir's friend Suraj Kumar had survived the battle and might still be living in Chandigarh. Military pension records confirmed a Major Suraj Kumar, decorated for gallantry during the 1962 conflict, residing at an address in Chandigarh's Sector 35.

Two days later, Arjun found himself outside a modest but well-maintained bungalow guareded by an fierce german shephard.

The man who answered the door bore little resemblance to the young soldier he must have been in 1962; his body now stooped with age, his face deeply lined his hair snow white. But his eyes remained sharp and assessing as he regarded Arjun's uniform.

"Major Kumar? I'm Captain Arjun Mehra. I've come about your friend, Havaldar Randhir Singh."

The elderly man's expression shifted from wariness to shock. "Randhir? After all these years?"

Inside, seated in a comfortable living room decorated with military memorabilia and family photographs, Suraj Kumar listened intently as Arjun explained his discovery of Randhir's remains and the subsequent journey to locate Leela.

"So she married a doctor," the old soldier mused when Arjun described meeting Priya. "Good. Randhir would have wanted that for her. He always said she deserved more than a farmer's son could offer."

"Major" Arjun amended, "I've been reviewing the records of Randhir's final mission, but there seem to be significant omissions. I promised his... Leela's daughter that I would try to discover the truth about how he died."

The elderly veteran studied him for a long moment before nodding slowly. "Some things remain classified, even after six decades. But perhaps enough time has passed."

Rising with the careful movements of advanced age, Suraj retrieved a worn leather folder from a locked cabinet. "My personal papers," he explained. "Including notes I made after the war, when memories were fresh."

For the next two hours, Arjun listened as Suraj recounted the events leading up to the Chinese attack; details absent from official records but preserved in the memory of a man who had lived with their consequences for a lifetime.

"Our commanding officer received intelligence about Chinese troop movements a week before the attack," Suraj explained. "He reported up the chain of command but was told to maintain position and avoid 'provocative actions' that might escalate tensions."

"Even though attack seemed imminent?"

"Delhi was in denial," Suraj said bluntly. "Political considerations outweighed military reality. We were ordered to report only through approved channels, using coded language that understated the threat."

"And Randhir's role?"

Suraj's expression grew solemn. "Three days before the attack, our radio operator intercepted Chinese communications indicating a major offense was imminent. Randhir, who had some knowledge of Mandarin from a language course during training, which helped in the translating. What we discovered was alarming; not just an attack on our position, but a coordinated offensive along the entire border."

"This information wasn't in any official report I saw," Arjun noted.

"Because it never reached headquarters through official channels," Suraj replied. "When our commander attempted to report, he was again told to avoid alarmist language. That's when he made a critical decision, to send messengers with the raw intelligence, bypassing the chain of command that was filtering information."

Understanding dawned on Arjun. "Randhir volunteered."

"We both did. I was assigned the southwest route toward the nearest Indian outpost, while Randhir took the more dangerous eastern path that might bypass Chinese advance positions. We each carried copies of the intercepted communications and our commander's assessment."

"He was trying to warn headquarters about the scale of the impending attack."

"Not just warn them; provide actionable intelligence that might have saved hundreds of lives," Suraj corrected. "The information he carried could have prompted reinforcements, evacuations of vulnerable positions, strategic repositioning. Instead..."

"Instead, he never made it through," Arjun finished quietly.

Suraj nodded his eyes distant with memory. "I barely survived myself. Took a bullet in the shoulder, nearly bled out before reaching the outpost. By then, the attack was already underway across multiple sectors. The warning came too late to make a difference."

"But you attempted to find him afterward?"

"When I recovered enough to walk, yes. Against orders." A spark of the young soldier he had once been flashed in Suraj's eyes. "I knew approximate coordinates of his intended route. Spent weeks searching after the ceasefire, until military police escorted me back to base."

From his folder, Suraj extracted a faded map with handwritten notations. "My search grid. I came within two kilometers of where you found him, based on the coordinates you provided. So close, yet..." He shook his head, six decades of regret evident in the gesture.

"The official report listed him as MIA," Arjun observed. "Nothing about his intelligence mission."

"After the war, there were... recriminations," Suraj explained carefully. "Questions about why our forces were so unprepared, why intelligence failed so completely. Acknowledging that frontline soldiers had identified the threat days before the attack, only to be ignored by higher command—it would have been politically problematic."

"So his true mission was classified, and he was simply listed among the missing."

"Politics," Suraj said, the single word heavy with disgust. "He died trying to prevent a disaster that cost hundreds of lives, and his sacrifice wasn't even acknowledged."

Arjun sat in silence, absorbing this revelation. The story was no longer simply about a love interrupted by war, but about a soldier who had died attempting to avert a national catastrophe; his actions buried in classified files to avoid embarrassing those whose decisions had contributed to the defeat.

"You know," Suraj continued after a moment, "he spoke of her sometimes. Leela. Never her full name, never details that might compromise her reputation if others overheard. But I knew she was more than just a village girl to him."

"What did he tell you?"

A smile softened Suraj's weathered features. "That he'd found someone who made him believe he could be more than his father's son following the same path generations had walked before. That she saw in him possibilities he hadn't imagined for himself."

He paused, his gaze turning inward. "The night before we left on our separate missions, he gave me a letter for her, in case he didn't return. But when I recovered from my injuries, his official status was 'missing, presumed captured.' There was hope he might be among prisoners eventually returned by China."

"You didn't deliver the letter?"

"I couldn't bring myself to," Suraj admitted. "Not when there was still possibility, however remote, that he might return. By the time it became clear no more prisoners would be repatriated, years had passed. I made inquiries about the schoolteacher's daughter but learned she had married and moved to Delhi."

He met Arjun's eyes directly. "I convinced myself it would be cruel to reopen that wound. Perhaps I was wrong."

"You made the decision you thought was right," Arjun said gently.

"Did I?" Suraj's voice carried the weight of decades of uncertainty. "Or was I simply avoiding a painful duty? I've asked myself that question for sixty years."

Before Arjun departed, Suraj made a request. "When they put Tiranga shroud over him, I'd like to be there. To stand for those who served with him, who knew his courage?"

"Of course," Arjun assured him. "It would be appropriate for you to speak, if you feel able."

"Oh, I'll speak," the old soldier said with sudden firmness. "After sixty years of official silence, I'll make damn sure his true service is acknowledged."

Back in Delhi, armed with Suraj's testimony and personal records, Arjun requested a meeting with the Director of Military Intelligence, an intimidating figure whose career had been built in shadows.

"This is highly irregular, Captain," the Director observed, reviewing the documents Arjun had submitted. "These events occurred before either of us was born. Why disturb settled history?"

"Because a soldier deserves recognition for his actual service," Arjun replied steadily. "Especially when that service was hidden for political convenience."

A long silence followed as the Director studied him with calculating eyes. "You understand the implications? Acknowledging that headquarters ignored clear intelligence warnings in 1962 raises questions about institutional failure at the highest levels."

"With respect, sir, those questions are historical now. The current leadership bears no responsibility for decisions made six decades ago."

The Director's expression remained unreadable. "What exactly are you requesting, Captain?"

"Declassification of records related specifically to Havaldar Randhir Singh's final mission. Recognition of his intelligence gathering role in his official service record. And permission for Major Kumar to speak candidly at the memorial service."

"For a single non-commissioned officer from a conflict most Indians have forgotten?"

"For a man who died trying to save his comrades," Arjun countered. "For the woman who loved him and never forgot him. For the truth, sir."

The following week brought provisional approval; limited declassification of records specific to Randhir's final orders, permission for his intelligence role to be acknowledged in the funeral service, and a commitment to review his case for possible posthumous commendation.

"The compromise of bureaucracy," Colonel Sharma commented when Arjun reported the outcome. "But more than I expected you'd achieve. Well done, Captain."

With military efficiency, arrangements for the memorial service proceeded rapidly. Havaldar Randhir Singh's remains would receive full military honours, with a ceremony at the National War Memorial followed by cremation according to hindu traditions. The date was set for the following Tuesday, exactly one week away.

Arjun personally contacted Priya to confirm the details, extending formal invitations to her family for the ceremony. Then, fulfilling the promise he had made, he visited her home to share what he had discovered about Randhir's final mission.

"So my mother was right," Priya said when he finished explaining Randhir's intelligence role. "She always believed he must have died doing something brave and significant."

"Brave, significant, and deliberately obscured," Arjun confirmed. "Politics overshadowed his sacrifice."

"And this friend; Suraj Kumar, he'll be attending?"

"Yes. He's elderly now but determined to honour Randhir's memory. I think meeting him might provide additional closure for your family. He knew Randhir personally, served alongside him."

Priya considered this. "I'd like my daughter to meet him. To hear first-hand about the man whose silver anklet I have inherited."

As Arjun prepared to leave, Priya handed him a small package wrapped in silk. "For the ceremony," she explained. "My mother would want this with him at the end."

Through the silk, Arjun felt the distinctive shape of the silver anklet, worn thin by decades against Leela's skin. The gesture moved him profoundly—this final reunion of lovers separated by war, politics, and time.

"Are you certain?" he asked. "It's been in your family for so long."

"My mother kept it as a connection to Randhir when she believed his body was lost forever," Priya explained. "Now that he's been found, it belongs with him. We'll keep his memory alive in other ways."

In the days before the ceremony, Arjun found himself oddly reluctant for his involvement in this story to end. What had begun as a simple recovery mission had evolved into a journey that had affected him personally, challenging his priorities and perspectives.

The love between Randhir and Leela; maintained despite separation, transcending conventional boundaries, and influencing lives decades later, represented something profound that had been missing from his own experience. His dedication to military service had left little room for deep personal connections, a choice he had never questioned until now.

As he prepared his uniform for the memorial service, polishing brass buttons to regulation shine, Arjun reflected on what would come after this mission concluded. Perhaps it was time to reconsider the solitary path he had chosen, to remain open to possibilities beyond the structured progression of his career.

Like the silver anklet that had connected two lovers across time and space, some stories continued to resonate long after their apparent conclusion. Some journeys, once begun, transformed the traveller in ways that couldn't be anticipated. Arjun sensed that his encounter with Randhir and Leela's enduring love had altered something essential within him, a change that would continue to unfold long after Havaldar Randhir Singh was finally laid to rest with the honour he deserved.

10

The Silver Thread

Dawn broke over Delhi with uncharacteristic gentleness for March, the harsh spring heat tempered by clouds gathering on the horizon. Weather forecasts predicted unseasonal rain by afternoon; the earliest harbinger of monsoon still months away.

In his quarters, Captain Arjun Mehra completed the final adjustments to his ceremonial uniform. Today would mark the culmination of a journey that had begun with his discovery of Havaldar Randhir Singh's remains and had led him through decades of history and the intricacies of a love story that had outlasted its participants.

The memorial service was scheduled for eleven o'clock at the National War Memorial, where Randhir's name would join thousands of others who had given their lives in service to the nation. His remains, transported with full military protocol from the mountain base where they had been temporarily housed, now rested in a simple casket draped with the Indian flag.

As Arjun arrived at the memorial, he noted the surprisingly large attendance. Beyond the expected military contingent; an honour guard, representatives from Randhir's regiment, senior officers including Colonel Sharma, civilians gathered in respectful clusters. News of the discovery of a soldier missing for sixty-three years had captured public imagination, with several media outlets covering the story.

Among the assembled mourners, Arjun easily identified Priya Kapoor and her family—her daughter Anjali, home from medical school in Chandigarh; her son Rohan with his wife; her brother Vikram, who had flown in from Boston. They stood together, three generations connected to a man none of them had ever met but whose influence had shaped their family history.

Nearby, supported by his grandson, stood Suraj Kumar in his ceremonial uniform adorned with medals earned over a distinguished military career. Despite his advanced age and the emotional weight of the occasion, he maintained the erect posture ingrained by decades of service.

Although it felt incomplete to Arjun as he could'nt locate Randhir's younger brothers and sisters

The ceremony proceeded with military precision. The chaplain offered prayers according to Hindu tradition, acknowledging Randhir's faith. Senior officers spoke of sacrifice and duty, their formal words elevated by the gravitas of the setting.

When Arjun's turn came to address the gathering, he stepped forward with the quiet confidence that characterized his professional demeanour.

"Havaldar Randhir Singh's story is both unique and universal," he began. "Unique in the extraordinary circumstances of his discovery after sixty-three years, universal in his commitment to duty and country that connects all who serve."

He continued with a brief account of finding Randhir's remains and the metal box that had preserved his final letter, carefully avoiding details that might intrude on the privacy of the Kapoor family. Then, with the Director of Military Intelligence's grudging permission, he addressed the previously classified aspects of Randhir's final mission.

"Recently declassified records confirm that Havaldar Singh died while attempting to deliver critical intelligence that might have saved countless lives," Arjun stated. "His actions exemplified the highest traditions of the Indian Army, courage and selfless service."

As Arjun concluded his remarks, he noticed Priya wiping tears from her eyes, her daughter's arm protectively around her shoulders. Whatever private emotions they experienced remained dignified, contained within the strength of family bonds that had accommodated Randhir's memory for decades.

When Suraj Kumar rose to speak, a respectful hush fell over the gathering. His voice, though weakened by age, carried the authority of first-hand witness.

"I knew Randhir Singh," he began simply. "We served together, fought together, and on that final day, attempted to complete the same mission along different paths. He did not return. I did, carrying wounds that healed and memories that never have."

With remarkable clarity, Suraj described the young man he had known; intelligent, thoughtful, devoted to duty but dreaming of a different future after his service concluded. He spoke of Randhir's courage in volunteering for the dangerous mission, his determination to deliver information that might save their comrades.

"For sixty years, I have lived with the knowledge that his sacrifice remained unacknowledged in official records," Suraj stated, his gaze directed toward the senior officers present. "Today, that omission is finally corrected. Today, Havaldar Randhir Singh takes his rightful place among India's honored martyr's"

As Suraj returned to his seat, aided by his grandson, the first drops of rain began to fall— gentle, hesitant touches against the stone memorial. By the time the honour guard stepped forward for the rifle salute, the rain had steadied into a persistent shower.

Following military tradition, the folded flag from Randhir's casket was presented to his next of kin. In the absence of direct family members, Colonel Sharma had authorized its presentation to Priya Kapoor as Leela's representative. Arjun, designated to perform this duty, approached her with measured steps.

"On behalf of a grateful nation," he recited the traditional words, placing the precisely folded triangle of fabric in her hands.

Priya accepted the flag with quiet dignity, her eyes meeting Arjun's in shared understanding of the moment's significance. Behind them, the honour guard's rifles cracked in salute, the sound echoing across the memorial grounds.

As the ceremony concluded, guests moved toward the reception area, where photographs and artifacts from Randhir's service would be displayed. Among these items, arranged by Arjun with careful attention to both historical accuracy and personal sensitivity, was a special exhibition documenting the discovery of Randhir's remains and the story of his final mission.

In a glass case, protected from environmental damage, laid the letter that had never reached its intended recipient; Randhir's eloquent expression of love for Leela, written hours before his death. Beside it, with the Kapoor family's permission, rested selections from Leela's annual letters to Randhir, spanning sixty years of faithful correspondence to a man long absent but never forgotten.

Central to the display stood a photograph of young Leela wearing the silver anklet during the monsoon dance that had become pivotal in their relationship. Beside it, a recent family photograph showed Priya with her mother in the final year of Leela's life, three generations of women connected by the story that had begun in a village near Amritsar more than six decades earlier.

In accordance with Hindu tradition, Randhir's remains would be cremated later that day in a private ceremony attended only by military representatives and the Kapoor family. But before that final ritual, Arjun had one more duty to perform, one not prescribed by military protocol but promised to Priya.

As guests dispersed, moving between the exhibition and refreshments, Arjun approached the Kapoor family where they stood with Suraj Kumar. The elderly veteran was sharing personal memories of Randhir with Priya's daughter Anjali, who listened with intense interest to first-hand accounts of the man whose silver anklet would eventually become her inheritance.

"Dr. Kapoor," Arjun said quietly, addressing Priya. "If you and your family would follow me, there's a private moment arranged before the cremation."

He led them to a small anteroom where Randhir's casket had been placed. Colonel Sharma, understanding the unique circumstances of this case, had authorized a brief private viewing for the Kapoor family—an opportunity for closure not typically included in military funerals.

"I'll leave you for a few minutes," Arjun said, preparing to step outside.

"No," Priya responded firmly. "You've been integral to this journey, Captain Mehra. Please stay."

The casket was opened to reveal Randhir's remains, now carefully prepared for final rituals. Decades in the mountain ice had preserved recognizable features, creating an uncanny bridge across time; the young soldier who had written so eloquently of his love for Leela still discernible in death.

Priya approached first, her professional medical training evident in her composed demeanour despite the emotional weight of the moment. From her purse, she withdrew two items—the silk-wrapped anklet and her mother's final letter to Randhir.

"My mother wrote to you every year," she said softly to the still figure. "This was her last letter, completed weeks before her death. She would want you to have it now."

With gentle movements, she placed the letter in the casket beside Randhir. Then, unwrapping the silver anklet, she held it to the light. The tiny bells caught the illumination, seeming to capture sixty years of history in their delicate curves.

"This connected you across decades," Priya continued. "My mother wore it every day of her life after you gave it to her. Now it returns to you, completing the circle."

She carefully placed the anklet near Randhir's hand, positioning it so the bells rested against his fingers; a final touch between lovers separated by war, time, and circumstance.

Each family member approached in turn. Anjali, the granddaughter who had never known Leela's first love but had grown up with his story as part of her family heritage. Vikram, who had travelled from America to honour the man who had indirectly shaped his mother's life. Their presence acknowledged the profound impact of Randhir's brief life on generations that followed his death.

When the family stepped back, Suraj Kumar moved forward with halting steps, his grandson supporting his elbow. The old soldier stood silent for a long moment, gazing at the face of his friend for the first time in more than six decades.

"I searched for you," he said finally, his voice thick with emotion. "Came so close. All these years, I've carried that failure."

He straightened to attention, offering a perfect military salute despite his age and infirmity. "Journey well, my friend. Your mission is complete at last."

As the private viewing concluded and preparations began for the cremation ceremony, the rain outside intensified unusually heavy for March, reminiscent of monsoon showers still months away. The silver anklet, restored to its original owner, laid silent now, its music stilled after decades of constant movement against Leela's skin.

Later that afternoon, as Randhir's ashes were collected for distribution according to Hindu traditions, Priya stepped forward and collected some ashes in to the urn where leela's ashes resided, thus fulfilling his promise of coming back to her.

The rain continued to fall steadily, creating a gentle percussion on the roof that reminded him of something Arju had read in Randhir's letter, the sound of rain on tin while Leela danced wearing the silver anklet for the first time.

"The rain," Anjali observed quietly. "Grandmother would say it's auspicious. She always said their best moments happened during rainfall."

"The monsoon dance," Arjun replied with a nod. "When he gave her the anklet."

"You've become quite knowledgeable about our family history, Captain," Priya noted with a small smile.

"It's been... more than a mission," Arjun admitted. "Following their story has affected me personally."

The cremation complete, Colonel Sharma approached with the official certificate documenting the military honours accorded to Havaldar Randhir Singh. "The museum display will become permanent," he informed Priya. "With your family's continued permission for the personal items to be exhibited."

"Of course," she agreed. "My mother would want their story preserved."

As the formal proceedings concluded, the rain began to ease, sunlight breaking through clouds to create momentary rainbows against the darkened sky. Military personnel and family members prepared to depart, the extraordinary funeral service of a soldier lost for sixty-three years now complete.

Before leaving, Suraj Kumar approached Arjun, his weathered hand extended in gratitude. "You've done what I couldn't," the elderly veteran said. "Brought him home, honored his sacrifice, and completed his story."

"Not alone," Arjun demurred. "You kept his memory alive all these years."

"What will you do now, Captain?" Suraj asked. "After such a mission?"

The question echoed Arjun's own recent thoughts. What did come after immersion in a love story that had transcended conventional boundaries of time and circumstance? How one return to ordinary military duties did after witnessing the extraordinary impact of two lives briefly connected but eternally influential?

"I'm not entirely sure," Arjun admitted. "This experience has... shifted something fundamental in my perspective."

Nearby, Priya was speaking with Colonel Sharma, likely expressing appreciation for the military's respectful handling of this unique situation. Her daughter Anjali stood slightly apart, her gaze directed toward the clearing sky, perhaps contemplating the grandmother she had known and the man whose existence had influenced her family in ways both subtle and profound.

In the weeks and months that followed, the story of Havaldar Randhir Singh and Leela Sharma captured public imagination. Media coverage of the military funeral led to feature articles exploring their love story across six decades. A documentary filmmaker approached the Kapoor family for permission to create a more comprehensive telling, promising to honour both Leela's relationship with Randhir and her subsequent life with Dr. Rajiv Kapoor.

Military cadets began leaving flowers at Randhir's memorial, inspired by the dedication that had led Captain Arjun Mehra to trace the journey of a letter never delivered. The silver anklet, reunited with its original owner after sixty years on Leela's ankle, became symbolic of connections that transcend physical separation.

For Arjun, the conclusion of this mission marked a beginning rather than an end. The profound impact of Randhir and Leela's story; its themes of enduring love, honour, and the capacity of the human heart to accommodate complex emotions, continued to resonate in his thoughts and choices.

Three months after the funeral, he submitted a request for transfer to a teaching position at the Military Academy. After fifteen years of active service, primarily in remote border postings, he found himself drawn to sharing the values and lessons he had gleaned from his career with new generations of officers. His experiences with Randhir's story had reinforced his belief in the importance of the human dimension of military service, the personal stories that lay beneath official records and regulations.

He maintained contact with the Kapoor family, particularly with Priya, who shared occasional updates about the on-going impact of her mother's story. When the permanent museum exhibit about Randhir and Leela opened six months later, Arjun attended the private viewing alongside the family, now connected to them by the unique journey they had shared.

As rain fell softly outside the museum windows; a proper monsoon shower this time, Arjun paused before the display case containing photographs of the silver anklet. The tiny bells that had once made music against Leela's skin as she danced in the rain with her first love were silent now, their story told through images and text that could only hint at the depth of connection they represented.

Anjali Kapoor, Priya's daughter and Leela's granddaughter, stood beside him, studying the display with thoughtful eyes that reminded Arjun of the photograph of young Leela.

"My grandmother told me once that true love doesn't always follow the path we expect," she said quietly. "That sometimes its greatest gift is showing us possibilities beyond what we've imagined for ourselves."

Arjun nodded, understanding that this wisdom applied not only to the extraordinary love story they were commemorating but to all lives touched by it; including his own. In recovering Randhir's remains and tracing Leela's journey through the decades, he had discovered something essential about what gives life its deepest meaning.

Across time and separation, through war and peace, despite barriers of caste and circumstance, Randhir and Leela's connection had remained unbroken; a silver thread weaving through generations, creating ripples of influence that continued long after both were gone.

As the familiar sounds of rainfall created gentle music against the museum roof, Arjun thought of the silver anklet now at rest after decades of movement. Like the tiny bells that had accompanied Leela through her journey, some stories continue to resonate long after their ending, their melody carried forward in the lives of those who hear them.

In a mountain battle six decades earlier, a young soldier had fallen while trying to save his comrades. In a village dance before that, he had placed a family heirloom around the ankle of the woman he loved. Neither could have imagined how their brief connection would echo through time; honouring both what was lost and what was found in its place.

The silver anklet had completed its journey, returning to its original owner after decades of faithful service as a tangible connection between separated lovers. But the story it represented continued, carried now in the hearts and memories of all who encountered it, a testimony to love's capacity to transcend the boundaries of time, circumstance, and even death itself.

-----------*----------*----------*----------